Ratwarmer

David Macpherson

Ratwarmer

Copyright 2023 David Macpherson

All rights are reserved

The cover Image was licensed through Canva

100pagedash.wordpress.com

On facebook David's group is Dave Macpherson is a Writing Stuff.

Instagram DavidScottMacpherson

One

The body dropped. A dead body to worry about, fresh and current. They didn't call me. I was in the station house, talking to Burt, the desk sergeant, when the call came in. Fisk and Maddin took the call and waved me off. "No Timmy, it's not anything for you. Don't you worry. Let the real cops police it up. We can get this one from evidence. We don't need it from the horse's mouth."

They had forensics do their lab thing. They checked for shell casings and blood spatter and they didn't call me. Nobody called me. I was telling Burt about samurai swords. The History Channel did a show on them and I was paying attention and got a lot of important facts. I was understanding what was important to tell him. I was ount of information That's what Burt was calling me: a fount of information. Not for my job, I guess. Just on katanas and tantos. Those are samurai swords. They are used for different jobs. But you don't need to know that now. Maybe later, I will tell you.

I was drinking enough sludgy police house coffee to keep me up until the coma hours and still do a hell of a great job, but they didn't call me. They didn't even give me a hint. I was in the office. I was right there.

It was a quiet month, all month and the one time they needed me. I mean really needed me and they didn't call. If they don't like me or don't like the idea of a ratwarmer, well I guess I won't be invited out for drinks. Which I am not. They don't want to drink with no ratwarmer. But the thing is, they don't need to like me to have me do my job. The city pays for me to be there. I even got a title that isn't ratwarmer. They have me on the books as a witnessing victim consultant. I guess that's a good way to describe me.

I like it better than being a ratwarmer. Though the thing is, I might like it better but I don't ever call myself it. Can you see me sidle up to the bar and say, "I'm a witnessing victim consultant for the PD, want to hear some fascinating anecdotes?"

So I kind of stick to ratwarmer. It means nothing. It's just words crushed together. Like homebase or walky-talky. Someone who sings against the bad guys is a rat. Kind of weird that a rat is the thing that sings. But that's always been the parlance for the snitch. It is a rat. It is a thing that sings. I've been to New York City and I have seen big economy sized rats. Though all my time there, I never heard one of them carry a tune. And the warmer part of the word? I guess it's because the corpse is still warm. Ratwarmer. Not a great name. I would ignore me too.

I got a call the next morning, I was still sleeping and the phone rang. It was Peters from The Current. Peters had been to the bar with me. Even wrote a feature on me. I clipped it. I have the yellowing thing somewhere around here. I know I should have it saved in a scrapbook, but it's the only story about me, so it would be a pretty sad lonely collection of clippings. Blank pages as far as the finger can flip.

"Tim, you son of a bitch, why didn't you call me?"

I was weirded out by this, Peters is a gruff reporter guy who even wears a fedora. It doesn't make much sense, but it's a badge to show what he does for a living. "What are you talking about? You told me not to call for no reason."

He snorted. "Really? I was under the belief that there was an understanding between the two of us."

We sure had an understanding. I let him know about the dead bodies that I get to tell their last breath memories and he accidentally drops a twenty or fifty on the ground for me to pick up. I know, kind of lame, but I was giving him nice information. He was just being forgetful in dropping his money in the most appreciative way possible. "I didn't not tell you nothing," I said. I was groggy and full of useless dream memories, but I was pretty sure I didn't have anything for him.

"Oh. You didn't. You didn't not tell me nothing about Mrs. Dominick Shtudt getting shot five times and dumped. There might not be a crime scene. She might have been dumped or she might have been there. It's a big headline mess and they don't even know the actual crime scene location and you didn't call me? What kind of friend are you Timmy? Next time you look down on the ground, the only thing you're going to find is you untied shoelaces."

He hung up on me. He had this anger on me and I didn't know nothing. This is not me acting dumb. This is me being plain dumb. Tim, in his natural state. At least dumb about the murder that went down. How could I call him about the tip when no one had me wired into it?

I ran some toothpaste around my front teeth and patted my hair down with water, knowing that both activities were little help to improve my presentability. I was rolling out of bed, not knowing what was going on. How Shtudt's wife was dead and me not making her sing, if I could. Maybe they didn't need me, like they said the night before. Maybe I was not needed at all.

I got to the station and wedged through news reporters and camera people, careful not to talk to no one or fumble over any power cord the camera guys were tripwiring the ground with. I thought my cousin's kids leaving their toys all over the place was like a demilitarized zone.. They had nothing on these camera folk.

I saw Peters, my now gone benefactor, and he just shook his head and gave me his back.

Getting through the door and flashing my laminate I saw Burt clocking out. He was in his civilian coat, though he still had his uniform on under it. "Burt, what's the deal? Should I have been here for this? Is this a big deal?"

Burt looked over his shoulder at the throng of media and handholding needs. He was looking to see if some coast was clear of something. "You don't want this, Tim. This is big."

"So why didn't they want me? They not warming the body? They not getting her to sing?"

Burt leaned into me, while still heading to the door. "Oh they will want her to sing. Sing bright and clear. Arias. Just not with you. They're getting Holbright. The guy from New York. They're getting the biggest name in Ratwarming."

He buttoned up his coat and said one more thing before hitting the outside, "They want someone who can get results. Not you, Tim. Not you." In my head, when I remember him saying it to me, I hear him with a thick Irish accent like all the desk sergeants had in the movies. But Burt had no accent. Maybe I remember it that way, not to make what he said any nicer, but at least it was a more melodic slap in the face. A beautiful, soaring sting.

Two

I didn't want to bring the dead back to life. That was not the plan. That was not the dream. It wasn't even the damned nightmare. My life was not great back then, but if I was told that I could have a steady income and all I needed to do was learn how to reanimate corpses, I would say no thanks and cross the street fast like that, with me not looking back.

I had a few bad years. I was a few bad years. I was a lot of bad decisions. Actually, I was a lot of no decisions at all.

I was not homeless, but I was making money like some homeless folk I knew. They were my competition for returnables. I had a shopping cart and I loaded that bastard up five or six times a day with beer bottles and soda cans. I knew where to go to get them. We all did, but I was a little more driven and got to those trash cans faster than the others. I had rent to pay in this manner. A steady form of income, but not an easy one. There was no slacking off.

I was good for seventy to eighty bucks a day. Fifteen hundred returnables a day. People who say that living down in the trenches is easy living are idiots. I was focused and my body was tight. Can't be pushing shopping carts all day and fighting for dumpster dominance and not be developing muscle groups and keen eyes.

Then the FlipSwitch. The FlipSwitch. The bartender at O. Onions, Liam, describes it the same way every time when he has a notion to talk about it, "The FlipSwitch. Where some people got some powers." That's a way of saying it. Bartenders are good with words, better than they are with cocktails in particular cases. Words make everything they describe taste right. I like how he puts it. Why try to make my own? That's work I don't need to do.

Lot of folk got stupid powers that don't do nothing. I know a guy who works at a McDonald's who walks into the room and the lights flicker. Just a little. Lights flicker. That's his power. Big nothing. There are mind-readers and spoon-benders and plant growers and there are reanimators. Not Zombie Kings, don't bring that term up. I ain't a king of nothing. And zombie, We bring dead people back, but there isn't a lot of lumbering monsters looking for brains. And let's be fair, most of us don't have a lot of the juice. That kind of power? Who even wants that kind of power?

There isn't a lot of folk who can bring back an army of the undead. There is a guy who drinks at O'. Onions named Mr. Winderston who, they say, can make an entire cemetery get up and boogie. That's what they say at any rate, no one knows that for sure. He's too nice a guy to do such a thing. He's a real gentleman, Mr. Winderston, and gentleman don't reanimate hundreds of corpses just to have a midnight rave.

And there is me. I got the juice. A little of it. I can bring humans back. Not for long. That is some hard work. I get knife-in-the-brain headaches after a long bout of reanimating. I can do it for a while, but I rather not be throwing up the night away from the pain.

When it first happened and everyone was talking FlipSwitch all the time, I wasn't going to do none of it. Cash in on it, I mean. None of that for me, thanks. I just wanted to have my apartment and my all weather job. It wasn't a great way to live. But I was living, you know? Like all of us, I was registered with the Man. They knew my power from the FlipSwitch. There was a top secret, never to be divulged, list. Yeah, everyone with a little scratch looked at that list. Someone had a look at the list, and offered me a job. I could have said no. I didn't say no. It was this job. This thing I was doing now.

Here is how it works, I suppose. I get the call and go to the morgue or the crime scene sometimes. I don't drive so a cop picks me up or I just wander over. I get an uber. I bum a ride. I get to where the dead are hanging about. I bring the dead back. Not a lot. I don't bring back the whole body. I am wiped out when I bring back the whole hog, the entire body. Even if it was easy for me, I wouldn't. It's not necessary and it freaks out everyone around too much.

I just need them to sing. Sing out the last few minutes. I bring back the head. It's a strange image, a moving animated head with shocked searching eyes attached to a dead husk of a body. Then comes the hard part. The impossible part: having the reanimated head say what we want them to say. That's the skill I don't think anyone can do. When the dead come back, they have a lot to say, but nothing we want. It's their dime. Their moment in the sun, once more. The walking off into one more sunset. They do what they want.

It can go like this, leaning up against my shoulder, the cop asks who killed you and then he asks it again and again until the reanimated head is aware of the question, or any human voice saying anything. Then the now alive head might say, "Who killed me, killed me, krill me, shrimp, lobster. Who broke my shell? Shell we leave this place? Yes, let us leave. Leaves. Leaf. Leap. For Joy. It's a boy."

That's the kind of nonsense they say. Course that's the kind of nonsense I hear at O. Onions at closing time from the regulars, so who is really to say what is reanimated gibbering and what is drunken confessions?

It's not an easy task for the cop to ask the right question and then get the right association. And because of all that, they say that it's the fault of the ratwarmer. They say the ratwarmer is to blame. That we are the ones that make it so hard to get a right word out of them.

That's madness. Ratwarmers are the ones that are even giving them the opportunity to get more information. It is not accepted in court. But we can get a good piece from time to time. It's a shot in the dark that is happening for no other reason than we got the juice. We got the power. The damned dirty gift.

I usually can't get the reanimated to say, "Why yes, thank you for asking. The person who hit me over the head repeatedly with that tire iron was my brother Joey. Joey did it."

Actually, I wouldn't want them to name someone right out, because they probably are thinking of something else. There is that nasty case of one of the first ratwarmers that got the victim to say that it was Tommy. It was Tommy. And there was a Tommy who was a suspect. After a year in jail, another guy confessed to the crime, and the reanimated corpse saying Tommy was a stream of consciousness response to The Who. You know, the band. The Who had an album called Tommy. And in it is the line, Hear Me. See Me and the Ratwarmer used those words to focus his gift and bring the guy back. He didn't mean to make the corpse think of the album Tommy, but that's what we think happened. And the guy Tommy spent a year in jail. You can't trust the words of newly brought back dead guys, I suppose.

Can't trust the word of the cops who hire you either.

I was hired for PR, I guess. What low level reanimator wants to do a useless, impossible task? Get Tim. Tim will do that dumb thing that amazes the rubes and don't really help the law and order one bit. .

Hell, I was hired by the PR division of the police. I am not even part of the investigators. The guys at the podiums decided that they wanted a FlipSwitch guy to do something FlipSwitchy. Mind readers were found to be against the fifth amendment. That's pretty stupid in my view. Every person incriminates themselves in their thoughts. If you can hear those thoughts, then it is fair game. Right? Easy pickings. The way things go.

The real cops wanted my gift to work, a little. Once they found that it didn't work as good as the ad copy on the packaging said, they gave me the cold shoulder. But the PR people must have a hell of a lot of sway because I was on the big cases. The whodunits. The headscratchers. Sometimes things came out that helped. I am sure of it. I know of three cases that closed because of the ratwarming I did.

I hope so at any rate. I was being paid to bring people back to help the common good. To get justice. Wish it was as easy as that. But I was being paid for it, and I didn't need to be treated like such garbage. Like a tossed aside food wrapper.

Of course the only person being tossed aside, really, was the victim. Mrs. Dominick Shtudt.

What a terrible thing to call her that. To not even have her own first name. It was Agatha.

When I knew her, it was Agatha Ulster.

But that was a long time ago. When all of us were young. And alive.

Three

As soon as I got into the station I took the back stairs to the third floor. There was an elevator, but I was told that that was just for officers and VIPs, I was a guy who was told to take the stairs. That's okay. I would have gone the stair route anyway, good for the heart. Good for the brooding thoughts.

I opened the door to Community Relations. Brian Palace was on the phone. He had a stack of post its with phone numbers. All the people who wanted to speak to the police about the killing. It was a real story and Brian was the one man in the office.

He saw me and I think he swore softly, because he then said to the person on the phone, "No, not to you, Sir. Of course not. I just banged my knee and it smarted. Hope you don't mind." He glowered and I am sure it was to me, this time.

The conversation happened as he hung up the phone and dialed the next one of the list. It took twenty minutes to have the conversation. Brian stopped in mid-sentence when he started dialing and then he picked it up right from where he stopped like there wasn't a long useless PR conversation wedged in the middle.

"The hell do you want right now Tim. This is crazed all hands time, ya know."

"If it's all hands time, why are my hands free and doing nothing?"

"Wanna pitch in, Tim? Wanna help with the big struggle? You got a pass on this one. No ratwarming for you. You can stay home. Wish I had one. But you got no horse in this race, lucky you."

"Why don't I? There is a whodunit. There is a famous dead person. You got a ratwarmer. You got me. And I was told to go home, And now I hear you are bringing in another ratwarmer."

"Heard that?"

"Holbright. You are bringing in Holbright. That guy on the late night TV. He's a damned charlatan."

"And what are you Timmy? You spinning a couple yarns yourself."

"No. I don't give false hope. I bring them back. They talk. We get what we can get. That's not being a hoaxster. That is being a guy paid to do a job and doing it."

"Some job. You are a line item from my department and what do you do? You don't look good on camera. You don't speak well to reporters. You give us nothing. How am I supposed to use that for PR? How am I supposed to utilize that for anything?"

"I am no faker."

"I don't care if you are fake or not, I want you good for the department. I want people to think that we are doing everything we can to solve murders. I want people to know we are embracing the FlipSwitch and we are using what we can from it. The proper use of technology. Fingerprints. DNA testing. Ratwarming. Things we can use."

"So you want a fake guy. A guy who is just a confidence man."

"A confidence man that wears a good suit instead of it wearing him. Yeah. I want him"

"Why are you bringing him in?"

"We're not, the victim's husband. He's bringing in the big guns. Who are we to say no? Hell, he might show us all how ratwarming is supposed to be."

"Great. Can't wait. Am I fired?"

"Fired? I don't know. I don't think so. Not right now anyway. We need you to be working with Holbright."

"I thought you said I wasn't needed."

"I did say that. I meant it too. I got the higherups wanting you but I was hoping you wouldn't be around for me to tell you. I was hoping to forget to tell you. You're like gum on a shoe. We need to have you show him the situation, to ask for help in a tricky problem. It's better for the spin that way. I might have said you weren't needed on this one, and that's pretty true. You just have to stand and pretend to be helping. Better to work collaboratively than have one zombie king push out another zombie king."

That's a nasty term, a term I was hoping to not use here, but I wasn't the one to be saying it. "That's a bad thing to say. That's an insult."

Palace looked at me without going back to the phone. "If you say so."

Four

Fisk was a big bull of a cop.

His partner, Maddin was bigger. He was fat. He wouldn't pass no health test, good thing he didn't have to. The union was good for that. He had chins for his chins. He drummed large round fingers that looked like chopped up snakes.

Maddin was working the phone at his desk. He was old school and worked the old heavy black phone instead of a cell phone. He probably couldn't navigate a touch screen with those overstuffed fingers.

So I was going to talk to Fisk. I walked over and got his attention and only his. I didn't say nothing. I didn't want to be more of a presence then just being there. Standing there like a target. I was still in the hall, not in the pen where the desks and phones were. Both could have seen me. I guess I was lucky there.

Fisk saw me and grunted a sigh. "Son of a." He looked at his partner who was into his phone call.

"A favor," is what I said. Just that. Not that I was going to get anything like a favor from him or anyone else. I didn't really say that. I mouthed it.

Maybe he didn't understand what my lips were forming but he pushed himself up and walked to the hall. "Coffee. That's what I need," he said to Maddin, who made like he didn't hear. No one seemed to hear. No one seemed to notice anything, I guess.

He walked right by me. His shoulder pushed me around in a half circle. Don't ask if I think that was intentional.

He went into the kitchen area and no one was there. I got there by the time he was putting non-dairy powder into his coffee. Fisk rolled his eyes at me. "What. And quick."

I was unsure of what I wanted to say, and now I was given just a short time slot to get everything I needed to say said. I hemmed. I grabbed at my collar.

"Dammit, Tim. Now."

"You are going to use Holbright? Holbright? He has an informercial on TV for people to learn about the life after death. An infomercial. That's better than me?"

"Nah. It's not better than you. I always thought you was useless anyway, Tim. Totally useless. But you are our useless. I don't have to go to New York to get a big pile of no help whatsoever, not when I can get that right here. This was not my call. The husband, Shtudt, wanted it. He insisted."

"He ain't a cop."

"So says the guy who ain't a cop neither. He has pull. We don't want to think that money factors in on an investigation, and damned if it should. But come on. They want this ratwarmer and only this ratwarmer."

"I don't like that term."

"I really don't care."

"But I can do as crappy a job as he can."

"Jesus, Tim. Look at yourself. You need to brush your head. You need brush your teeth. You need to look less like a welfare hotel guy. This guy Holbright has suits and a smile that I'm sure was worked on by a dentist. You ain't got it. You are going to be standing next to him from what I hear. He is being a liaison and you are the contact. All smoke and mirrors. So get some clean clothes. Move up your shower schedule."

"It's not going to help Agatha, a well dressed ratwarmer. Not going to help her at all."

"Agatha. Wait. Who the hell are you talking about?"

I turned my head away. Looking at the wall. Looking at the fact that I spoke too much. "What? That's her name," I mumbled. "Just thinking about the victim. Like we're supposed to. Like you guys always tell me to."

Fisk stroked his mustache. He looked at his belly. Not as big as his partner's gut, but big enough to gaze on when thinking thoughts.

"Tim. If you know this girl. This dead body. Pretty girl. Looked good on Shtudt's arm. Not great dead. But if you knew her when she was cute and breathing. If you know something. Tim. You need to give."

I didn't hesitate. I just spoke. "Heard her name was Agatha. Though everyone is calling her Mrs. Not her name. Thought that was wrong. That's all."

"I ain't talking to you. I ain't bothering, Timmy. But you need to read the file, much as I don't think you should. You need to know about it. This Holbright is coming. You should have a little knowledge when you talk to that well-dressed charlatan." He tossed his coffee cup into the trash and kept on talking to me as he walked away. I knew not to follow. "Don't get the file from me. Get it from Burt, he has a redacted copy for you. If you have problems with the big words, ask him. Leave us alone. You ain't being generous. You know something. And that's not good, Tim. You knowing something is not good."

Five

Don't get me wrong. There is a lot that isn't bad about the job of ratwarmer. Let's just be fair, it's ratwarmer. That's what I was. Nothing fancy with a lot of words and syllables. Ratwarmer. The rat was me. That was nothing to be upset about. A word and a word and a word, make three words and three words don't make enough to buy a stale donut.

There were a few things that I liked about the job that didn't help law enforcement. The best thing was the paycheck. I was paid decent. Money in my pocket. Money in my pocket was food in my belly. Not crappy food from the discount center. I was having a reuben with extra Russian dressing at Murry's. My fingers were sticky and orange and I was feeling okay for the first time that day.

I had a cup of coffee, in a real mug, which was a nice thing about Murry's. I was feeling like a well heeled man, eating elegance, instead of the useless also ran that I truly was.

It gave me the courage to read the file on Agatha. Not much of a file. It was just three pages. It was the day-log of the event. The real report would be coming. Hell, by the time I was eating this, the file was no doubt multiplying in an unruly mess of paper.

It was nice to have only three pages. I wasn't good at a big file, not that I had cause to look at one too much. I read it and stained every corner of every page with Russian dressing. I didn't even touch some of them.

Agatha was found in an alley behind the Parker Hotel on Temperance. The town has a couple streets with dive bars and seedy shops, but nothing was seedier than Temperance Lane. If I was to be asked, I would say the bars settled there just because of its name. Dive bars are nasty like that. They always wind up where they are least expected or wanted. It was less dive bar haven then shooting gallery for dopers and tweekers and the flippers. Thank god reanimators don't attract the flippers. We don't have the power they get jonesed on.

They get a nasty high from the FlipSwitch folk doing things to them. Some think it's some sexual kink but the word started coming round that it was a habit. That it was a dependency thing. Junkies I can understand. I don't like them, but I can understand it a little. But getting a fix from a FlipSwitcher? That stuff is madness lost in stupid weird.

I had a flipper following me around once. That lasted as long as when she saw me entering O. Onions, the bar where the reanimators drink and the flipper was annoyed. She swore at me, called me a zombie king good for nothing and walked on by. I guess no one can get a high from reanimating dead people. I know I don't.

I stopped losing track of my thoughts and focused my eyes back to the page. Agatha was shot five times. Most in her back. She seemed to be strangled with a rope or something. There were signs of it, I guess. The words the forensics people use are there just to confuse the rubes in the cheap seats. She had a rope or something around her neck, and that's all you need to know. Actually we needed to know a lot more. Like why was she there in that alley. Why strangle and shoot?

A paragraph went into the "curious" lack of blood. There was indication that the crime happened in the alley. From her scratches and torn clothes corresponding to items in the area. But where the hell was the blood? Five bullets. That should have been a given. The guys think she was moved, but didn't want to push all their chips in. They were hedging. They were confused. It was a nice feeling to realize I wasn't the only one.

There was a summary of an interview with Dominick Shtudt, her husband. He was at a business dinner for the evening and then took in a show with a potential investor. I don't know what a potential investor is. Is that a guy who might give money for your latest skyscraper or is it someone with the possibility of getting money somewhere down the line. A big shot wannabe.

Shtudt took the money guy, or possible money guy, to a cabaret. Who has cabarets? I didn't know there was anything like that anymore.

I thought that the only place with cabarets is TV shows set in the fifties and sixties. I thought they were set pieces for old time shows. And to have a cabaret in our city. That didn't seem possible.

Shtudt was asked about his wife, which is fair because she was the one who got killed. She was at the house at the Swallows when he left for the night. Of course the house was at the Swallows. Gates and guards. It would look swanky and upscale if anyone was allowed to look at them. Shtudt stated she never came to these events and was staying home. She stayed home a lot. She did community work with the LGBTQ community, specifically with homeless issues with that population. That was nice, though I don't know why it made it to this initial report, like it was amazing she did charity work. Or maybe it was the type of charity work.

A quick call to the guards at the Swallows gate said that her car didn't go through. She made no calls. There was nothing on the video to show her coming and going. Agatha lived in a house that was a dead area for surveillance. Most of the houses and streets had cameras but the most exclusive area in the Swallows, the Back Lane, had none. More privacy. No one needs to worry about what goes on in those houses. Don't worry your little head about it.

The file should have more things in it. But it didn't. I was given at least something to look at. Something to make myself feel a part of the team. My sandwich was gone. I was still hungry. I was still wanting. I got two coffee rolls and had them put in a bag. I had to get ready. I was to meet up with a celebrity ratwarmer. I was to meet and greet with Holbright at five o'clock. I was to be his happy gladhander at the airport. Like I was a chauffeur holding a cardboard sign with the name "Holbright" magic markered on it.

Six

I went to the apartment and tried to look like a guy who should be picking up a celebrity at the airport. Well, he had a TV show, but I wouldn't have called him famous. A lot of people stumble into TV shows. I watched a lot of History Channel and Home Shopping Network and there are people who seem as shocked to be on TV as much as we are aghast watching them.

I showered, brushed my hair and teeth. I uncovered my "ready for a funeral" clothes and put them on. They showed themselves to be roomier than the last time I wore them. I put on my regular shoes, because why should I be that uncomfortable?

I stopped, figuring that I needed my watch. My watch was what I wore to let people know I was serious. It was also nice to find out the time.

I scooped it up from the top of my dresser. I clasped it to my wrist and saw the photograph of my sister placed in a resting picture frame. She was holding hands with Agatha in the pic. Agatha's head was resting on Kathy's shoulder. They were young there. They will always be young now. Two dead women. A title to a picture that didn't need to be named.

The last time I saw Agatha was right before the FlipSwitch. She was already married to Shtudt and she found me on the street while I was rooting for cans to cash. She was doing volunteer nonsense. Helping the helpless. She was shocked to see me, though she kept her press conference smile on as much as she could. She insisted on taking me out to dinner, like it was going to be my first decent meal in years, or maybe it was a last meal before the chair.

We talked about old times. Which was the times she was with Kathy. We talked about Kathy like she didn't die at twenty two. Polite conversation never brings back dead loved ones. We got mad at each other when the bill came. I insisted on paying. I could pay. So I was going to pay. I was not charity. I was not a project. "I ain't destitute, Aggy. I am poor. I reek of dumpster. But I can pay for some sandwiches. Now just smile and accept it. I do myself fair.."

I didn't see her after that. I looked at the watch again, still lost in useless memory. She gave me that watch. Kathy said it was from her for Christmas, but we all knew who picked it out. Not Kathy. I took off the watch and left it on the dresser. I picked up the picture of Aggy and Kathy, folded it and put it in my pocket.

I didn't go straight to the airport. The Public Relations arranged for a car. Actually, it was one of the cars from the Studt Organization. So I haggled for them to meet me at O. Onions. I didn't really feel like them knowing where I lived. I didn't want my address to be part of the Shtudt record of the investigation. Better for them to know where my bar was.

I didn't get tight at O. Onions, just a few shots and a beer to even me out. Liam, the bartender, wanted to know why I was clean and presentable, "I'm not against you wearing such an attire, but it's something I can't get my head around. Is this showing respect at a wake kind of deal? Is someone dead?"

"Someone is always dead." I finished my drink and went to the front door. I stopped, pulled out the photo of my dead sister and her now dead friend. I ripped it into eights and dropped them into the trash. I waited out front for the car to pick me up. It was already there. Expectant. .

Seven

Holbright was big. He took up the entire backseat of the car. Not really, but it felt like it. He was waving arms and loud voice. That was big enough to push me out of the frame. His publicist rode up front with the driver.

I was in the back with the man, the Ratwarmer. He wasn't ashamed to say that. "We are ratwarmers. It's just a name. It's up to people like us, to our talent and skill to make people realize that it is a good word. They hear ratwarmer and they are happy and relieved. They know that justice is coming. The ratwarmer has arrived, the bad guy will now be caught."

The publicist laughed right on cue. She said, "Good one. And so true." She took out a notebook and wrote something.

"Is she writing what you just said," I said in a stage whisper. I didn't mean to speak that way, but it's the only way I know how to whisper. I was never good at stealth.

Holbright bellowed a laugh. A big laugh for a big guy. He wasn't fat. Just big. Shoulders and chin. His hair was big too, like a televangelist on a public access station. His voice rattled the windows. I'm sure it wasn't the wind. It was his damned, too big for real life voice. "I hope she isn't writing down my every word. Not my every word. Sometimes I ask for a tissue or where the bathroom is. I don't need to have my every word written. Not those."

It was definite. I hated him.

He shooed away something, like a fly or a bad stench. "I'm just kidding. She tries to come up with something useful. I don't give a lot of useful sound bites, sad to say. The reality is, it is hard to sell what we do. Of course, when we do sell it, it is worth it. Justice and truth."

"You get them to sing?" I asked. I figured I might get something out of him.

"Sing? Who sings? I once sang in dinner theater. But that was the before time. That was hungry days. It was a good voice, I grant you. But it was a hungry voice."

There was a pause. He wasn't going to say anything more. "The dead. When you reanimate them. How do you get them to speak clearly and help with the investigation? Like in the TV show, with your recreations."

He smiled. "TV. The producers didn't want them to speak like they do. They said that it's disturbing. I didn't believe them. I wanted it all to be as accurate as possible. I'm not a liar, after all. I held my ground. I insisted they speak the way they do in real life, when they get their real life back. That free association. I felt we were doing a disservice to the art by not being accurate. The producers played my version to a sample audience. They hated it. They hated the reanimated. They hated me. They found the way they spoke. Well, disturbing."

"That's a way of putting it. It's not reassuring."

He leaned into me, he seemed angry. His face was tight and coloring pink. "What are you talking about? It is nothing but reassuring. What can be more reassuring than the dead opening up their eyes and talking? What does that say about the universe that we can make that happen? We. You and I. We make that happen. How can that not be reassuring. They are not opening their eyes. Them not speaking, speaking anything. That's not reassuring. We are never going to find the truth if they are dumb and dead."

"How do you find the truth? They talk crazy talk? They talk nothing we need."

"Tim, are you telling me that your work hasn't helped the force?"

"Well, sure. A couple times. A word or two reminded the detective about something and he changed his investigation and we got the guy. Couple times. But no easy answers. No set responses."

"Where's the fun if they just said, I know who did it? Where's the joy in that? Tim. You are out here in the sticks. Don't misunderstand. It's a city we are in. I can tell. There are highways and high-rises. You have a city. But forgive me if I say this, you are being too provincial in your thinking. Don't think of it as free association, as crazy talk, as recently dead banter. Think of it as Jazz, think of it as taking a theme, a set of notes and keys, and running with it. We are not reanimators at this point, we are conductors of the most out there jazz orchestra."

"Is this the new thing for your TV show? They are scat singers that need to be analyzed like a review in Jazz Monthly?"

Holbright laughed, "I didn't know there were jazz magazines anymore. I thought it was all websites and Twitter reviews."

"I just made it up. Do I look like a reader of jazz magazines?" I was getting angry and I couldn't do anything but sit and watch my responses leave my mouth.

"No Tim. You look like someone who is a walking accident."

"I'm an accident waiting to happen? Is that it?"

"No. I didn't say that. I said you are a walking accident. You aren't going to get hit in a car wreck. You are the car wreck."

I went for the door, which was a dumb thing because the car was cruising forty miles an hour heading to the next red light.

Holbright patted my shoulder. "I don't need consoling," I said. "I just need you to not call me a wreck."

"Then what are you?" he asked in quiet tones. Like he was trying to coax an animal from the cage and out into the open so all the paying customers might see.

"A ratwarmer."

"And what does that mean?"

"Not a hell of a lot."

The rest of the ride was silent. The publicist in the front seat whispered into her cell phone and Holbright stared at his fingernails. I looked at the buildings, knowing that the morgue was coming. I was thinking about what he said. That the dead spoke in music. That they spoke a truth like a good melody is truth. A truth we might fight over, but it don't mean it isn't right.

I knew that soon we would go through reporters and Holbright would stop to give an impromptu speech that he had rehearsed on the plane coming here. How he was here just to help. That I was a talented ratwarmer who asked for his assistance, his guidance, as we are such good friends. But the time for talking should be short because Mrs. Dominic Shtudt required justice and we were to see if this could be done with her help. We were but servants. This, I figured was what that con artist Holbright would say. More blowing air, more words that should be seen more as music than meaning.

The publicist leaned back and smiled at me. It made me feel like I was watching a toothpaste commercial. "Don't misunderstand, Tim. We are happy to have you here. Any person who practices that art of ratwarming is a good thing. We will need you to sign a few forms, just in case we put you on one of our programs." She had a clipboard of papers ready for me.

I signed. Like a good boy.

"This is great," the publicist said. "Team work always looks good in the media. I'm Janice."

"Tim," I said. I grimaced when I said it. She was kind enough to not say, "I know."

We arrived at the morgue. The crowd swarmed the door. We got out and it happened like I supposed. It was no special power, it was just too damned obvious.

Eight

The first dead body I ever saw was my sister Kathy's. My sister the suicide. I was called to identify the body. It wasn't easy. The body was battered and bloated. Jumping from a bridge and then floating about for three days will do that. I said it was her. I'm sure it was. But I wasn't sure from looking at her. She had no tattoos or scars that I ever knew of. I said it was her, because, I just knew it was.

I hate to say this next part. I spent a lot of time wanting to talk to her after she died. I wanted to bring her back and ask her so many questions. A lot of questions. None of them would have been, "why." That's one I never felt bold enough to ask.

This was before the FlipSwitch. When I got my powers I thought of trying to find the remains of my sister. I had some talking to do. But she was cremated and there was nothing really to say.

I didn't want to do anything with the power. It was just part of the body. Like my brain has the ability to rattle off math problem, like 14 plus 28. Things like that. My brain can do that. But it doesn't really matter. I don't need to know 14 plus 28. That's how I felt about being a reanimator. Sure. I can bring the dead back. That's just ducky. How is that going to win me the girl and get me the car?

Then this job came about and now there was a purpose to me. I made the public think that reanimation was part of the public good. It helped solve crimes. What it really did for me was get me acquainted with the dead.

I have seen a lot of gone faces with nothing in them. There is something removed in those drained faces. That's what it seems like to me. So the question is, what am I doing when I am doing the reanimating thing? Am I finding the thing that is missing and putting it back? Am I giving some of mine, which seems a tad too generous to me. Or is it a different engine? Is it a piece of machinery none of us can understand? Is it the FlipSwitch messing with the concepts of life just to watch us freak out and lose faith in everything?

When it does happen, when we bring them back, life shows up in the cheeks. Life comes back in the skin, warming up quickly. Life comes back all over the place except for the eyes. The eyes are not absent eyes. They are the eyes of dead squirrels stuffed with sawdust and glued to a plaque for the wall. They glitter in the light and make you think they are alive. It's the lie of light.

It's the eyes that make you realize that this ain't going to be easy. That they are not going to get up and speak to you in a straight way. Those eyes tell you that nothing is an easy fix.

We strode into the morgue and Fisk and Maddin stood beside the draped body. Maddin mumbled, "Great, now there's two of these freaks."

Fisk mumbled back, "Shut up. Making this worse." He put on a smile so fake it had to be real in some drunken world. "Mr. Holbright, thank you so much for coming. Are you ready to do this? When Tim ran this racket, I mean, when he used the gift there was no run up. He just did it. Is that the same for you?"

"Are you in a hurry, detective?"

Fisk looked at Palace, who was haunting the doorway. "Ah the hell with it," Fisk said. "I ain't going to play nice with this ratwarmer, Palace, okay? Yes. Holbright. I am in a hurry. This case is now twenty hours old, a practical senior citizen, and I'm waiting for a damned FlipSwitcher to play hookum on the body. Yes I am in a hurry. I got a dead girl. I got everyone breathing down my neck for twenty hours and I don't even know where she got popped. Wasn't that alley. And now I got to dog and pony you idiots. Yes, I am in hurry. Do this dumb useless thing so me and my partner can go out and possibly do some policing. Alright?"

Maddin laughed so hard, he leaned forward. Not a big lean, his fat frame wouldn't allow a full bend over belly laugh. No way. "Who's playing hothead now?"

Holbright tinged pink. "I was asked by the victim's family to aid as I can. I do not need such comments. If done right, all assistance can be helpful. You must allow me and my team to do what we can."

Maddin wiped tears from his eyes. "So Tim, you are on his team? You are the relief pitcher of ratwarmers now?"

"I'm pitching clean-up for no one. I am here on the insistence of our department. Can't have New Yorkers coming in riding publicity mad roughshod on our patch." I had a memory of attending a double header baseball game with Kathy and Aggie. Two dead girls eating hotdogs and drinking cups of beer in a memory I planned to keep to myself.

Palace got all territorial as well and said, "That's right. Tim is here because we need him to be. We want to make sure that this guest is doing things by our procedures. It is nice to have a minor celebrity like yourself here Mr. Holbright, but we still are our own department and we like that. Our murder numbers are at a record low, something I don't think New York can say at the moment."

Holbright's publicist, Janice, hissed, "We can make this an issue with the media. And this is not a threat of a smear. I can just tell them exactly what you just said and all the papers will be screaming that you are fostering obstruction."

Maddin barked a laugh, "Obstruction my fat ass." This cracked up Fisk, which is what it was intended to do. "I apologize," Maddin gasped out. "Let's do this thing. I need Palace and you little Ms. Spinmeister to leave."

The publicist straightened with indignation, "You can't throw us out."

"I can. Because I have to. The fact that I want to toss you out is just gravy."

Fisk jumped in, "This ain't a circus. This is part of the investigation, and we have rules and regs. And what's the rule for this Tim?"

I bit my lip. I just loved being somebody's trained seal. Watch me balance the damn ball on my nose. "At the crime scene when there is a forced reanimated confession, there is only the facilitator and the detectives."

Maddin said soberly, "Let's not bring everyone in on this thing. This is delicate." Despite it all, I knew he meant it. A few times, after I released the corpse from reaminated life, and it was back to being empty, I caught the big cop leaning over and saying, "Sorry about that." I don't know if he wanted to keep that a secret, but I think it was best to play it that way.

Soon, it was just me, the detectives, and the telegenic Holbright without a camera in sight. "I was told that Mr. Shtudt, the grieving widower, wants to be here when I reanimate," Holbright pointed out, "I was informed he is on his way."

"Nuts," Fisk said.

"The hell with that," Maddin concurred. "Do it now, do it fast, get that damn thing over with or get the hell out."

"We need to do it after that, we have Tim," Fisk said. I don't know if that was a sign of respect or that they just hated Holbright a little more than they hated me. Either way. I'd take it.

Holbright sighed. "I'm not going to explain this to the grieving widower." He tensed his shoulders and his fingers jutted out like he was hit with a live wire jolt. He completely relaxed and exhaled slowly and loud. What the hell was this, I wondered. Why is he making a show? He should just look at the corpse and it's alive. Was this still more flash paper and hidden mirrors nonsense?

I looked at Agatha. Her empty shell. The eyes slammed open and I knew something was up. They looked like eyes and not aggies in a marbles game. The head pitched forward to the chest. Without looking at anyone, Agatha, the dead victim said, "Tim. Tim? Are you there Tim? You have to help me. You brought me back, right? You brought me back. That's what you do. You bring back people shot dead. I've been shot dead. You have to help me Tim. I can't hear you Tim. I can't see. You are Tim, aren't you? Please say something Tim. Tim."

Nine

"Another."

"You just had a third, Tim. You see what I did there. I demonstrated the ability we bartenders have in paying attention to the alcohol consumed by our customers."

"Another."

"You don't seem to care about my bartending abilities. This hurts down deep. This makes me feel like a functionary in your eyes, instead of a real person, like I fancy myself being."

"Another."

"If you think repeating your request over and over will get you your fourth shot of Jack, then you are absolutely correct. I might even give you a fifth one. But the sixth shot is not even a possibility."

"Thanks."

"You can sip it there, my friend. You can enjoy the complex flavors, the textures."

"I'm drinking Jack Daniels. What complex flavors are you talking about, Liam?"

"I am dealing with a philistine. What about your friend over there? Does he need to abuse his alcohol like you are doing currently?"

"He's fine. He can sip and stare off into space like he's been doing for hours now. Let him."

"Why is everyone stealing looks at him? Did he say something wrong? Did he step in something foul?"

"Nah. He's kind of a big deal. He has a TV show. Can I get one more shot? I'll walk it back to the table. Promise."

"TV show? Really? How come I don't know him then?"

"It's not a really good TV show." As I carried my drink to the table where Holbright sat, I nodded to Liam. Which meant that he was going to put it on the tab for the end of the night. There were no freebies at O. Onions. But you didn't have to pay as you went. At least if Liam liked you, you didn't. It was a fine day when I graduated to "pay at the end of the night" status. I was finally somebody.

I sat down opposite Holbright. "Did you get me another?"

"No," I said, "you need to slow down. You need to pace yourself."

Holbright pursed his lips, as if he was mad at me. He blew out air. "Fine." He swigged at his beer. "How can this be? How can she talk like that? I never. Well. I have brought back a lot for their final words. And never."

"I know," I said. "You already said that. You said that at the morgue. You said that to Fisk and Maddin. Both at the station and at their bar. Why did you agree to go to a cop bar anyway?"

"We work with police, why wouldn't we go to their bar?" He seemed puzzled with the concept. He was puzzled by a lot of things.

"Because we are not cops. We are not anything like cops. We are ratwarmers. We are reanimators. We have our own bar. We drink with our own people. Are things so different in New York that you don't need your own bar?"

"I don't go to bars."

"Of course you don't." The alcohol was not hitting me in any way I liked. I was feeling numb. I was feeling antsy and I wanted to go to bed. Not to sleep. But to my small bed. Just so I had a place to be antsy by myself.

The cell phone in front of Holbright did the vibrating dance again. He didn't make a move for it. It wasn't my phone, so I didn't care too much. "That him?" I asked.

"Who?" he asked, staring at the movement of the phone on the table.

"Who? Are you really going there? The grieving widower. The guy with the money. Was it Shtudt that called? Come on now."

Holbright looked more annoyed than had been all night, which was saying a lot. That guy was very annoyed when he didn't get the photo ops he was expecting. "Of course it is him. Who else has been calling me all night? Of course it is him."

"You ain't answering him?"

Holbright looked at me like I just arrived. He looked at me like wires shocked him awake. "They are not supposed to do that. They have never done that. How can I work when the dead don't act like they are supposed to?"

"I think we need to talk to Mr. Winderston now." Holbright was against it every time I brought it up. He didn't like the idea of some reanimator from this backwash town being an expert in anything.

We didn't get a chance to fight and argue anymore. That was when Dominick Shtudt came into the bar.

Ten

He was a handsome man with a long straight chin. His eyes were large and light, like a kittens. His hair was perfectly manufactured on his head. The suit was beautiful. I know nothing about clothes or rich things, but this suit was beautiful Charcoal and soft.

He didn't seem happy walking into O. Onions. It wasn't a sneer he had. He was just very deliberate on where he put his feet and hands. He spotted Holbright and walked over. He took a chair from another table and placed it at the head of the booth. He sat down like he was being lowered by a hydraulic lift. He turned his head to Holbright, and said in a soft fluty voice, "My wife is dead and I paid a very hefty sum to have you here right away and you are sequestered away drinking beer in, what, a dive bar."

Holbright didn't speak. After too long a pause I chirped up, "Yup. That's where we are. He wasn't too hot after the weirdness happened." Sitting in a booth at O. Onion, in my bar, I was emboldened. What the hell? Why wouldn't I be? Everyone was being so quiet, like pauses were as good as discernible speech.

The rich man staring at me sighed. "I suppose I should wonder what that means."

"You should," I said. "She did something that I haven't seen done by a person brought back. Not like that. She was very clear and concise."

The man looked relieved when I said that. "So you have her saying what terrible thing occurred to her. To my wife. You have her clear and concise." He looked straight at Holbright, not me, but Holbright. The guy who cost him more money, that's the person Shtudt chose to look at.

"She didn't want to tell," Holbright said.

There was a pause as this settled in. There was a look of shock on the rich man's face. It was a look I was seeing of lot this evening. "What does that mean?" Shtudt said each word like he was pushing them out between gambler's lips.

"It means," Holbright said, losing all his glamor with each unpleasant phrase, "she knew she was dead and only wanted to speak to Tim here. She knows Tim. Knew Tim. None of us knew that fact. When Tim spoke to her. She didn't trust the others around. She said she wanted to speak to Tim alone. In private."

"Well," the husband asked, "why didn't you just leave and let this Tim speak to her in private like she asked?"

"He did," I said. "I mean, I did. It was me she was asking for. Least we could do was follow her wishes. Besides, the cops thought it was funny she wanted to talk to me alone. They were more than pleased to escort Holbright out and leave themselves. The thing is. When we were alone. She didn't say anything useful."

"She went back to gibberish? The gibberish you ratwarmers get?"

"No. She didn't say gibberish, Mr. Shtudt. She didn't say anything of the sort. She was just asking how I was. What I was doing with myself. Was I eating. And other things. Things I don't think you need to know."

The man stood halfway up, ready to fling himself at me, "How would you know what is important to me? My wife is dead and is now talking to you, you an unclean ratwarmer, and you get to decide what I need to know. Is that it?"

"I don't get why everyone is concerned with my cleanliness. I showered before I went to the morgue." I stood up, thinking about another drink. Though I doubted that Liam would allow me such a thing. I just needed to get away.

"No," Liam said.

"Just looking for another type of conversation," I said as I watched Shtudt and Holbright talking quietly but with angry motions and twisted mouths. I was sure that everything the husband needed to know, Holbright was giving.

"You got some company there, Tim," a voice said next to me. I looked and it was Tony. Tony was one of the best respected reanimators in town. He worked in the hospital. He reanimated people who just died so they can last a little longer and have their organs harvested. It was a respected job, for a reanimator at least. That job didn't have a nickname. No one called him a prolonger, or a harvester or nothing like that. They just said, Tony, he works at the hospital. He does good things for people. That's what they said about him. Not all of us had such luck.

"They ain't company. They just some people stuck to me like barnacles. Can't shake the rich and famous. That's my problem, Tony."

"Oh, you are such a beacon for the well to do. Shut up. Will you." Tony usually had a smile for everyone. He was a good guy, well adjusted, as much as anyone of us can pull off. He wasn't smiling. "Rich guy and a fame whore. Not the kind of clientele Liam usually allows into his shining castle on the hill."

"Yeah, they let people like me in. That's bad enough."

Tony was about to say something else, something of a different tone and tenor. I could tell by the way he shifted his weight and cleared his throat, as if to say, the fun preamble nonsense has ceased, now it's time for the grown-up talk.

But before a word came out, Holbright stumbled over. He said that he and Shtudt were leaving. They had things to discuss. The work wasn't over, and I was to meet him at the police station at eight in the morning. It was already one thirty. But that was okay, I wasn't going to sleep. Sleep was for the guiltless. I nodded and Holbright and the rich man left. As soon as the door closed, the entire bar seemed to exhale a long breath it had been keeping in for far too long.

Tony nodded to Liam, who smiled and poured a whiskey for me and beer for Tony. "I thought I was cut off."

"Well that was only if you were leaving at closing time in thirty minutes. But you are not leaving my young friend. You are staying here for after hours."

"You kick everyone out, I've seen it."

"Sometimes, Tim, sometimes I can get talked into inviting friends to stay and chat. Totally informal, and not completely illegal."

Tony smiled at that. "Mr. Winderston wants to talk to you."

Eleven

It wasn't long before the place was cleared for the night and I was still sitting there with a glass of good whiskey. What's good whiskey? I don't know. I couldn't taste anything different from the well bottle I usually paid for and drank. This was fancy stuff and I guess that was by the way smart folk stared at the bottle and whistled at the name. The good whiskey had nothing to do with taste for me, but for admiration in others. I suppose.

The only table without chairs upended on it was the one I sat in at the back. It was away from any prying eye on the street. Anyone peering in would have seen nothing but the fact that things must close and rest every day.

"Where's Mr. Winderston?" I asked. It was Tony, a guy named Marcus and Liam cleaning a pint glass with a wet rag.

"He's checking on a few thing," Tony said, "Our Mr. Winderston is a busy man."

"And an important one," Marcus added.

"Who cares if he is important?" I snapped. I was tired. I was wiped out and though at first I was pepped by finally being asked to eat Thanksgiving dinner at the grownups table. No more card table in the rumpus room for me, whatever the hell a rumpus room is. The shine was off for me. It was too late for me to be impressed by anything other than the simple solution of a warm, clean bed. "If he wants to talk to me, he should be talking to me. I like you, Tony, and I like the idea of getting the good drinks, though really, who cares. He should be talking to me."

"He is talking to you," Marcus said slowly, almost embarrassed. "He's listening." He pointed to his phone, which showed that it was on and connected.

"I get a disembodied voice? Great. What is he Charlie and I'm one of the damned angels. Am I Kate Smith?"

"I am impressed with your knowledge of old time television," Liam said, "but please be respectful. You know Mr. Winderston would be here if he could."

The phone crackled sound and Mr. Winderston phlegmy voice came through, "I'm at the office looking at some files. Files that I can only access at the site. I'm sorry Timothy."

"Tim. I don't know no Timothy."

The voice continued, "I was greatly aggrieved by what you reported of what the dear departed said."

"You and everyone else."

"You ever hear of anything like that?" Tony asked. "I have never heard of them talking other than cadaver speak."

"That's the name for it," I asked. "I didn't know there was a name for it. I just thought it was dead people nonsense. It has a name. Cadaver speak. Holbright thinks it is like jazz. That's improv based on something underneath."

"Holbright is an idiot. He likes the lights. He thinks everything is performing," Marcus mumbled. He was a little more caught by the whiskey than the others.

Tony went on, "Cadaver speak is the only way any of them talk. I don't know if that's the official term for it, but it's what I've been told it's called and that's all there is. There is no one getting up and talking straight and true."

"That's not completely accurate," the voice on the phone said.

Marcus and Tony looked at each other. Tony shook his head. He looked at the phone waiting for more words to appear.

"What's not completely accurate," I asked. "There's a lot of things about us raising the dead that doesn't seem accurate."

"We don't raise them, this ain't a horror movie," Marcus said, his voice rising.

"Come the hell on," I said. "We worried about names and labels? If I say zombie, you gonna throw me out of the bar?" This was a valid question. A lot of us hate the word zombie and O. Onions has a ban on saying it. Free speech and all that, but some people really hate that word. Like a word will bite you and turn you into a monster as well.

"Tim," Tony said quietly, "you are upset. You had a day I don't think I would ever dream of having or wanting. You had a bad day. From being pushed out by Holbright to the cadaver talking normally and asking for you. You can be mouthy all you want, but the thing is, you left the big question on the table."

"What?"

"What do you mean, Mr. Winderston, that's not accurate. That cadaver speak happens to everyone."

There was another long pause of nothing coming from the phone. "Sorry, I was looking for something. No, sorry Tony. I'm attempting to find some information. The truth is there is a class of people who don't emit cadaver speak. It's a small class and we have found a way to avoid having any of these cadavers used by reanimators. They are not used for road work, for organ donation, they are not allowed to interact with, uh, ratwarmers."

"Portuguese?" I asked.

"No," the voice from the phone said. "The Affected."

Marcus swore.

Tony whistled.

I shook my head and spoke my heart, "What the hell are you talking about. The infected? Infected with what?"

Marcus laughed. Nervous laughter, but I didn't care for it. I was laughed at too much, if anyone cared to ask me.

Tony said, "It's a term not a lot of people use. It's a government term. Affected. Affected by the FlipSwitch."

"All of these inaccurate terms," Mr. Winderston said. "All of these ridiculous titles. FlipSwitch. Ratwarmer. Reanimator. Ridiculous things we are forced to say."

I was pleased that he rambled on like that. It gave me a few moments to figure out what was said and what it meant. "Flipswitch folk don't talk crazy when they're brought back."

"Yes." I didn't know who said that. I looked up. It was Liam. The bartender. The only one with no powers. I guess he had the power of speech, something robbed from the others.

"That means Agatha Shtudt," I hated saying that last name for her, for Aggie, but I wanted to be clear. I wanted to be understood in all this confusion. "That means the girl, the cadaver, the one I and Holbright brought back, she was a FlipSwitch. She had a power."

"Yes." Liam again. He poured another whiskey and took it himself.

"What did she have?" I asked.

"How are we supposed to know," Marcus said, more puzzled than mean.

"She was a pre-cog," Mr. Winderston's voice. "She was level three. Not very strong. Could sense danger more than really see the future. Rated C"

"C level," Tony said, "not useful for society. The skill, not the person. The person can be useful. Just the skill isn't.."

"She didn't even have a good parlor trick to impress the neighbors," I said, "but she still had to carry around the card."

"You knew her right?" Marcus said. "That's what you said, you knew her. Did you know she was gifted by it?"

"I didn't know her now. I didn't know her now when they called her by her husbands name or when she could tell when a piano was going to fall from a high window. I didn't know any of her that way. I only knew her when she was a kid. When my sister was in love with her. And I guess she loved her too. That was the person I knew. Only her."

That killed the room. I had a gift to shut everyone up.

Tony was the first to start up again. He was pissed. "How were we not allowed to know this? This is important. That those who got the gifts act different in reanimation. What else is different about us?"

"What isn't?" Marcus said.

Mr. Winderston cleared his throat. "Do we really want the world to know that there are other aspects that make us strange? Freakish? We can avoid reanimating those who were gifted, then that's an easy fix. A simple solution to a problem. And it is a problem. Just look at how you all reacted to her reanimation. The hold was put on her being reanimated, which was why you were not called to be involved in the interrogation of the crime scene Timothy."

"Wait," I said. "I wasn't invited because it came up that she was one of us? A FlipSwitcher? So why did Shtudt get his wish and have Holbright reanimate?"

"Ah," the voice on the phone pined, "if only we had as strong and consistent control over the world as all the conspiracy theorists choose to believe. If only I could have stopped him from ever being a reanimator. Have you even seen what he calls his television show? Dreadful. We were overruled by money, a lot of money."

"Shtudt gave enough cash for you all to be ignored," I said.

"No," Mr. Winderson's voice said. "No. It wasn't him. That would require cash and from what we here at the office have been able to ascertain Shtudt was near bankrupt. Too much wild speculation on commercial real estate, or something to that effect. For the life of me, I don't understand how people with no money can still live an opulent life."

"Easy, no one ever wonders. They live on embers. Gas vapors. Call it living," I said to myself.

"Shtudt was in on it, obviously, but there was no way he could have paid for it. Something like that, greasing the powers that be and paying for Holbright to come immediately all must have been cash. A lost of cash."

"So despite his haircut," I said, "Shtudt might as well been collecting cans. Cutting coupons. Not raising any dead wife."

"The thing I don't get now," Tony said, "is who paid for it then? Did he know about what was going to happen? Did the money man know how the cadaver was going to talk?"

There was no time to answer that, if anyone had an answer. The door shook with large insistent knocking. "Who the hell?" Liam said as he walked over to shoo the noisemakers off.

"Bet you it is the cops." I mumbled. I was quiet, not to keep a secret but because I just didn't care to be loud and articulate. "Frisk and Maddin coming in to talk to me.

"Are you expecting someone to be arrested?" Tony asked.

"No," I said. "I'm expecting someone else to be dead."

Fisk and Maddin and poured drinks and tilted them back. They didn't ask for them, but no one was going to say no to them. "Timmy, we need you to do that hocus pocus crap we pay you for," Maddin said.

"Shtudt is dead," I said.

Fisk tilted his head. "How the hell did you know?"

"Aggie told me. When she spoke to me. When we ratwarmed her. She told me then."

Twelve

"It goes without saying that we should be doing the interrogation," Janice, Holbright's publicist said. Maybe she was his assistant. Maybe she was his boss. I never bothered to look at her before, but I was seeing her now like she had dropped from a ripped open cloud. She was small but put together. She radiated a sense of importance. Or maybe that was just what the alcohol in me was seeing. I was feeling the alcohol still from the afterhours sessions at O. Onions.

"It goes without saying?" Maddin asked Fisk. He didn't look at the woman. The woman who was stronger and more determined then the person I barely registered in the car.

"I don't know," Fisk said to his partner, still nothing to the woman. "It goes without saying that we have a murder, right?"

"Well, the ME hasn't said definitively. But that's MEs for you. They can't take a gift slit throat for granted," Maddin replied.

"Yeah, I can't get those lab coat types," Fisk replied. "They see a guy with his a new gap in his pretty neck and wonders, could this be a tiny home accident? Lab coats, they are too careful for me."

"And too skinny," Maddin added. "What is it with those science types that make them skin and bones?"

"It's not natural. They can't be well rounded law enforcement entities with them showing much rib cage." The two cops laughed.

Maddin wiped his eyes and mumbled, "well rounded." He took a breath and asked, "But what about our Timmy here. He don't have an ounce of a fat on him. And we trust him."

"Yeah, I hear you. But look at Timmy. He's so pale and unhealthy. He's sickly. He don't have any pounds on him, but he looks like he is seconds away from kicking it. That has got to count for something." There was more laughter. I might have been insulted. I might have had a sense of pride that they once again included me in their struggle against the outside big wigs. But I felt seasick. I felt like I was another big wave from developing my sea legs, my new equilibrium.

Janice swore and then exhaled and put on a fake as you please smile of assurance. "Are you slabs of beef done? I want to know if you will let Mr. Holbright do what is right and get the confession of the victim. It's what he is here for."

Fisk said, "No. That is not what he is here for. Actually I don't know what the hell he is doing here anymore. He was supposed to get the testimony of the deceased Shtudt woman and that was one gigantic cock up. Turns out she only wanted to talk to Timmy. And talk she did. She even predicted that her husband was going to join her soon. Got to love heartfelt reunions. That's right Timmy, she predicted to you?"

I nodded.

Before the two police officers could continue with the banter they seemed to be enjoying rolling out, the woman raised her hand to yield. She was little, but that was a powerful gesture that quieted the room. "Mr. Holbright is one of the finest ratwarmers. He must do this."

"She called it ratwarming, that's a nasty invective, right?" Maddin asked me.

"I don't mind the term," I said.

Fisk shook his head. "Okay. This has been fun, but I am putting my big old fat foot down on this. And that means you too Maddin, let's get this thing moving along again. Miss. I am going to say no to your guy doing anything. I will let him and you stay, but that's about as far as I am going. That's me being nice. Now hold on. No one talk. Holbright was hired by Shtudt to ratwarm his wife. I think that was crap. I think that was publicity or a smoke screen or both. I don't know why he did it, but he did it. And he had himself some juice with the downtown cats, but that is as far as it goes. This is probably related, but it is still a separate case. I have no reason to extend the courtesy we were forced to give before. Like I said, you can stay, but if we want a testimony from him, we are going to use our sickly ratwarmer."

Maddin nodded, "In other words, you had a shot and you blew it. Now we are going to go with our weirdo. We like to keep our weirdo use in house."

Everyone looked at me, but Holbright. He wasn't looking at anyone. Janice was the one in charge. I didn't realize it before, but she was the one making things happen. Holbright was the puppet slid over the hand, nodding and clapping. "Fine," the woman said. "Fine. We will go to the press then. We will state clearly about the shoddy way you handle these tragedies."

"Tragedy?" Fisk said with rising anger. The word lasted several rising syllables. "Tragedy is a sad thing that could not be avoided. Tragedy is a busted furnace that poisons a family in their sleep. This ain't tragedy. This is a damned ugly murder. I don't care for you using happy little words, but don't misunderstand, this is nasty events that needs to stop. And go to the press. Spell my name right. Don't mess that up at least."

"We are done," Maddin said. "We are taking Tim in and he's going to do whatever he does. Probably nothing. Probably more wrong turns. I hate wrong turns. I hate wasting time and this conversation with this lousy coffee is nothing but a wrong turn."

He stood up. Put his hand on my shoulder and clasped it tightly. He raised me up and walked me to the door to the morgue. "Do whatever you do, Tim. Be quick with it. We need to get back to knocking on doors."

Thirteen

I was chilled in the room with the dead. They kept it cold. I felt colder than that. I thought the drink and the new found attitude I was trying out was going to keep toasty and warm, but I guess those false flames only go so far. In a room with dead people, that kind of heat is second class.

It was me and the detectives. I had Holbright with me. I requested assistance. I don't know why exactly I insisted, but I did. "The guy's throat was cut ear to ear, I might need help in getting him to sing. Hell, I don't know if he can sing and I can't change that." This was a lie. I was going to get him to talk. I just wanted that guy next to me. I wanted another person who might know what it feels like to do this kind of madness. This kind of magic trick.

I had to give it to Holbright, he was almost back to normal. His swagger was returning. "I could do this for you, Tim. I know that he was my employer, but maybe I should do it, more fitting."

I didn't say anything to that. Fisk filled in the silence with a question, "Are you second guessing letting the guy come in with us?"

"A little," I said. I was about to apologize to the New Yorker, but I looked up and saw him smiling. The limelighter wasn't worried about being insulted. He was just happy to be talked about. I was sure that the woman who managed him, Janice, would spin this to make him the hero of the day, savior of the neighborhood. Even if it wasn't ever his neighborhood.

The body cooled before me. The handsome man I saw at O. Onions, with is swagger and opulence was a pale, receding form. He wasn't anything of the guy I thought he was. He was dead, there wasn't anything of the guy I thought he was. He was a damned husk.

"Are you going to do it or not, Timmy?" Maddin asked, unknowingly tapping his foot to a nice beat.

"I already did it. He's back," I said.

Holbright leaned forward, "Wait, he's too still. He hasn't had the shock." That's what we reanimators called the moment when reanimation occurred. The corpses shot forward and immediately opened their eyes. There was no subtle reanimation. Or so the media ad copy would have anyone believe.

"The shock is for suckers," I said. I made the line count, but the truth was, I was surprised that he didn't shoot up. He was back, but just lying back and taking it easy. I was not going to show my hand. I wasn't going to tell no one that this was not part of the plan. Let them think I have super powers. Actually, to most folk in the world, I did have super powers, just none that anyone wanted.

This guy, this Dominic Shtudt, this great man so he says, slid into reanimation. He was dead and then he was kind of not dead. He was awoken gently. He stirred. The muscles on his left shoulder twitched like a fly had landed there. His eyes didn't open. The eyelids fluttered for a moment, but decided to stick to that. He made a wheezing sound that seemed to be more morning yawn than a scream of terror.

"This is not what I expected," the mouth of Dominic Shtudt said. The quality of the voice was of a quiet buzz, a saxophone warming up with long notes. Not an improvised melody, just a long breath of possible music.

"Dammit," Fisk said, "another one talking like people talk."

"It's a surprising development," Holbright said. I realized he was going to jaw longer about that, but I batted that nonsense away with a glare and a wave.

"This is not what you expected," I said.

"No, not what I expected at all."

'You can open your eyes," I said.

"I can open my eyes. I can." He didn't open his eyes.

"You can open your eyes and see what is around you."

"Why." He said it not as a question. I wasn't sure he had the ability to create that kind of inflection, if he wanted to make it a question. He was too dead for such distinctions. "Why? I would see people standing over me. And poor ceiling panels. Must I see things I care not to see?"

"I don't care. Open your eyes. Close your eyes. I really don't care. Do you know what's happening?"

"I'm dead."

"That you are."

"You can understand me."

"We all can. You are speaking clear and easy."

"Dead people don't speak easy. Dead people don't make sense when they talk," the dead person pointed out.

"Yeah, well I think you got a little secret you didn't let anyone know."

"What secret, we all have secrets."

"Dammit, Shtudt, I don't want to have witty goddam banter. I just want to get moving and help to slam cases closed."

"Amen to that," Maddin said

"You got yourself a gift from the FlipSwitch," I said. "What is it?"

"I was not killed because of a gift."

"You a police detective? You know what's important?" I asked.

"You ain't a police detective neither," Maddin said quietly.

"Tell me what your gift was," I said ignoring the police peanut gallery of comments.

"Influence."

"The hell you say, that's not a gift. That's just power."

"And power is not a gift?"

"There is no influence gift on the registry," I said wearily. I was getting a runaround from a dead guy. And the strain of keeping him back and talking was pulling at my braIn.

"You have influence, you can make sure you are not any list."

"Let me get this straight, you had the power to convince people to do things. To make things happen."

"Yes."

"And people with influence can get that kept off the registry of gifts."

"Yes."

"Did this influence power get you killed?"

"No."

"Who killed you."

"A man with a knife."

"God dammit!" Fisk shouted. He leaned forward, I thought he might be trying to hit Shtudt, to get him to talk. Strong arming a dead man who doesn't care about any kind of arms, strong or not.

I raised my hand. Yeah. I raised my hand like I was a grade schooler. Fisk saw it and nodded. He sat down again. "I'm not used to dead guys giving me lip. I don't like it from people with pulses, you think I like it from corpses?"

"I am not sure. I don't know you well enough," the dead man said.

"Let me," I said. I raised my voice, "A man with a knife killed you."

"Yes."

"Do you know the name of the man with the knife?"

"No."

"The man with the knife, you never saw him before."

"The man with the knife. I did see him before."

"Where did you see the man with the knife before?"

"He was opening the car door for Walter Benfress."

"He worked for Walter Benfress."

"I don't know."

"But he opened the car door for Walter Benfress."

"Yes."

I leaned back and said, "Who the hell is Walter Benfress? That's important right?"

Fisk and Maddin looked at each other like I said something stupid. I didn't know what I said, but it didn't feel like something stupid. Of course that's always what a stupid person would think.

"I even know who Walter Benfress is," Holbright said. "He is a venture capitalist."

"Nah," Fisk said, "he's a guy on a tv show. They let poor schlubs go on and show them their inventions and this guy and other guys decide if they want to buy it and sell the things. Dumb things, like singing shower heads and junk like that."

"The money ain't a joke though, the money Benfress and them are throwing around," Maddin said.

"Money guy," I said, "got it. Could have just told me that. There is a lot of people with money I don't know, so you don't have to rub my nose in it." I leaned into the corpse. I was getting pretty tired. The reanimation taxed me and I was sweating. "Okay," I said to the corpse, "okay now. What were you doing with Benfress?"

"Business."

"That's a non-answer, of course you were doing business. What business were you doing."

"Marketing a pill."
"Was he putting the money up for the pill," I asked.
"Yes. he was putting the money up for the pill."
"What was the pill?"
"It was called pill."
Fisk swore and said, "This has got to be going somewhere very fast."

I nodded. "Why was the pill called pill." I heard what I said and almost laughed out loud. I knew this was serious, but I was saying the word pill a lot. I was beginning to miss the free association speak of the normal reanimated.

"It didn't have a name yet. I wasn't worried about the name. It was going to get a name by those who bought it, those who sold it." The dead voice seemed annoyed that I didn't understand him. Even the dead thought I was thick.

"The pill was being made from something else, something we already know."

"Yes."

"What was the pill being made from?"

"Sky-fi."

I looked at the cops and they shrugged. I looked at Holbright and he was shaking his head vigorously. Not the shaking head of someone who doesn't know and answer, but someone who doesn't want to believe what he was just hearing. "What?" I asked him.

"There is no such thing as sky-fi," Holbright said loudly.

The corpse heard this and said, "There is such a thing as sky-fi."

"A damned myth, not real," Holbright said.

The corpse didn't seem to worry about Holbright. He paused, like corpses tend to do, and continued. "Sky-fi is a street name for an increasingly popular street drug that has some of the rush of crystal meth, in addition to the hallucinogenic effects of organics such as mushrooms. Some have described it as coked up peyote. The mortality rate is one in two thousand, and the addictive quality is moderate, which makes it a very valid business model."

"If it's so awesome a hit," I asked, "why is it that me and the cops in the room ain't never heard of it. If cops don't know it, then it don't exist. That's a standard law of nature."

"Amen to that," Fisk said.

"The issue with sky-fi is that it's a difficult drug to use in its current marketable state."

"Pulling teeth here Shtudt, you are like pulling teeth."

"I have all my teeth, no one pulled them. Have they been pulled since I was killed."

"Don't tempt me," Fisk said.

"Why is it not marketable? Sky-fi, why isn't it bigger. What's with its profile?"

"Currently, it is the blood of the gifted, mixed with distilled vinegar."

"Jesus," Fisk whispered.

"That's messed up," Maddin added.

"That's not true," Holbright shouted. "That is just not true. Isn't it tough enough to be us. To be gifted? Are we to be thought of us the way to get high? To get buzzed? That is just not true."

"How," I started to ask the corpse. I stopped. I thought to ask it again. I couldn't. I walked over to Holbright. "I don't care if you say it isn't true. Let's just say that it is," I whispered to the famous ratwarmer. "Let's just say it is and that you know about it, because you do. Now tell me without any hems or haws or in betweens. Tell me. As far as you know, how the hell do they get the blood? Our blood. Dammit. How."

Holbright gave a sour look and gave it up. "Down and out flipswitchers, they give it up. Like the red cross. They bleed it into a bag. It's mixed and then it's shot up. That's what I've been hearing from the outer boroughs. They say it's a thing. I don't. I can't. No."

I walked over to Studt and slapped the dead face. I slapped it again. I kept him alive, I didn't wipe the spark from him. I kept him alive as I slapped him. Not that he felt it. We are pretty sure they don't feel it. But I did. My palm stung as I slapped him one more useless time.

Fourteen

Mr. Winderston was there in a half hour. He was big. He was the guy who knew things about the world we live in. He worked for the government. He was the government for all I knew. I was the one that put Shtudt back on ice and called him.

"I have heard it by a few names, Loll, Blodip and a few others that will disappear," Mr. Winderston said, "but Sky-fi. That's such a terrible name, it will no doubt stick."

The cops were upset. They were calling me weak for wanting to get Mr. Winderston in. They wanted nothing to do with expert FlipSwitchers. This was still a goddamn police matter. Not something for the tabloids or In Search Of. But I knew what I was dealing with here. Actually, I didn't know any bit of what I was dealing with. Call in the expert. Call in the marines. Call in a guy who never seemed shocked or put upon. Call in the guy not like me. I might pretend to be in control, but I was shaken. Hell, it took three times for me to press the right buttons to get Mr. Winderston.

Mr. Winderston looked fatter than I ever saw him. I only saw him at O. Onions before this. Maybe a bar slims a guy down. His suit fit him better than the suits in a men's magazine. It looked perfect for him, like all the skinny guys wearing gray suits had it all wrong. His hair was cut neat and his mustache was full and slightly aimed down, the most discrete of handlebars. He took possession of the center of the room. He was the right gravitational middle of the universe.

"Is he still reanimated?" he asked me.

"Are you kidding? I pulled it away as soon as he told us what the drug was made of. Are you kidding? Do I want anything to still be animated if I have a say in it, which I do."

"Let's not talk about the body, moving around or dead like he should be," Fisk said. "How can we not know of this drug? This is a drug from FlipSwitcher's blood for God's sake. Blood. How are they getting the blood? Do we have a murder spree on our hands that we know bupkis about."

Mr WInderston looked over at the police men. "That's very sweet of you to say. To think that the law will know about the new FlipSwitch drug. Or shall I amend that and say the latest FlipSwitch. Sky-fi is the first to elicit a narcotic effect from the blood. Bottle Cap was a drug mixing the skin of FlipSwitch individuals and methamphetamine. It had strong results, but the mortality rate was not fiscally feasible. You never heard of it because it was chalked up as a bad batch of meth. We, those that knew of such things, helped with that deception."

"Bottle Cap," Fisk repeated. "That's one dumb name."

"For a killer, indeed it is," Mr. Winderston said. "Trunk was nasty, if I am allowed to say. It was generated from the vitreous humor. That is the fluid of the eye. It was mixed with cheap brandy. It gave a slight sense of aphasia. It didn't work correctly for those drinking it."

"Sounds like a great Saturday night," Fisk said.

"The high wasn't worth the four hours of vomiting afterwards. It was shunned by those that should have loved it. There were others, but Bottle Cap and Trunk were the most troublesome. Sky-fi was popular and it didn't seem to have an issue with mortality or excessive vomiting for that point."

"They were going to make a pill of it," Fisk said.

"So Timothy informed me. That was something I was not aware of. Which is why I have come. I have questions for the deceased. From Shtudt. I shall ask him a few more questions and then you can get more details to assist in his murder. But I will want to talk to him first."

"Uhm," I said, "Mr. Winderston, you can't. I tapped him already."

"I'm sorry, Timothy, I am not familiar with that term."

"I brought him up and then pulled it away. That's being tapped. Tapped. The keg is dry, you can't bring him back. I know I should have kept him cooking, but the whole thing made me gooseflesh all over and I let him slip down."

Mr. Winderston laughed a little. He stopped, realizing that he was laughing at me, and not with me. "Sorry," he said. Sure, he laughed at me, but he apologized, which was something I didn't get much of. "I guess some reanimators can't do multiple callings."

Holbright was annoyed and said, "Not some. No one can. I never heard of anyone calling up the dead twice. I know of one guy who said he could, said he was the only yo-yo reanimator, but come on. There is just too much fantasy and make believe going on here."

"You are right Mr. Holbright. There is too much fantasy going on here, so I will only talk the hard facts. It is seven in the morning and none of us have slept, so I am sure no one wants make believe anywhere near this event. I must say that being yo-yo reanimator is a terribly funny thing to be. Especially if he is a ratwarming yo-yo reanimator. Imagine how he would walk the dog, go around the moon, make the cradle. That's what it's called, right? Make the cradle?"

"Rock the baby, Mr. Winderston," I corrected. "And you have lost your train of thought," I corrected some more.

"Indeed. Some people can bring back the dead multiple times. Usually, it can only be done on a corpse once. There is too much stress on the nervous system for it to spark again. But then, there are some few who can modulate that spark. One can be frugal with the flow of the gift. Whatever that gift might be."

He walked into the room where the dead man was. We all followed. There seemed to be no rules or hierarchy at this point. He put his hand on the dead man's forehead. He looked back at me, "There is no reason to touch the corpse. None whatsoever. But I find that this contact makes more sense aesthetically, and that seems to aide in my control."

Shtudt's eye's opened. "I am here."

"I know," Mr. Winderston said.

"I shouldn't be here. I was called up once."

The large man paused. "How do you know that? How do you have that memory?"

The dead thing smiled. "Things are different. Aren't they?" The two police detectives stepped back like someone pulled a gun.

"What did you do to your wife," I said, I couldn't help myself. Mr. Winderston shook his head disapprovingly.

"She didn't like what was going on. She went to talk to someone. She was light headed." The damned thing laughed and laughed and blood seeped from his eyes. His body twitched and contracted and anything that might had been considered life was gone from the husk. The bastard was more dead than most.

"That did not go in any expected manner," Mr. Winderston said.

Fifteen

There was too much mystery. There was too many fantastical things. We didn't live in a crazy fantasy world. We had expectations that things happened in the way things happened. Sure, since the FlipSwitch, the whole idea of rational expectations changed, but they were still the rational explanations. There was corpses not talking clearly and in a coherent fashion. There was the reality that revived corpses do not allow themselves to explode and turn into a running mess. Even with bringing back the dead, things happen like in any ordinary world. It's a new ordinary world, but it is still ordinary. At least until the next shift, the next FlipSwitch, but we can't expect that. We have to live in the now.

So for the now, I had enough.

I walked out of the room with people calling my name.

I went home.

I went to bed.

I slept for ten hours. I unplugged the phone. I still believed in landline phones, primarily because they can be unplugged. The new world of cell phones allowed too many ways to stay attached. I had a cell phone, but I didn't know where it was.

I was alone and no one could reach me.

That wasn't true, someone slamming their fist on my door could reach me. And that's why I slept for ten hours and not for longer.

I could have slept for days and the whole thing would have blown over. Here's the thing. I was never the hero. I was never the guy to solve the big mystery, if there was going to be such a useless duo as mystery and solution. Who the hell needs such things. You get paychecks, you get complimentary booze, you get a place to sleep. That's all I ever was and am. Who killed Agatha, who killed Shtudt, who spread the Sky-Fi pill and all the ins and outs and the conspiracy and the headlines for those who still insist on reading newspapers.

With me involved in the whole mess, it was resolved in three days. If I wasn't involved in the mess, it still would be done in three. I was never important to the story. The big story. The thing I'm doing here, is telling my story. The one that matters to no one but me and maybe a few dead women: Agatha and my sister.

I don't know that for sure. Don't test me. Don't bring out a slide rule and measure the reality and the world without me. Don't do any of that. Just trust me for once.

Sixteen

She slammed a fist on my door, smearing it red with blood. It was okay. It wasn't hers. I let her in. I insisted that she go and wash up.

"You think that there won't be more blood all over this place?" Janice asked.

"I don't care. If you need bandages, I have them."

"I'm not cut."

:"Then whose blood was it?"

She grinned and her smile took up her whole face. "Holbright's." She was compact. She had a big smile. She had a big gun. It was pointed at me.

"Why did you kill Holbright? Now you are out of a job."

"He was just a way into the FlipSwitch community. He really was a hack. Do you think I thought his show was worth my effort? No. But he had blood he didn't even know he was giving to us. And he knew a lot of other FlipSwitchers. He was a means to an end."

"You paid for him to come here and you were hoping to clean up the mess."

She gave me an okay sign with her hand. "You are not as dumb as I thought."

"I am pretty dumb if I let you make a bloody disaster of my apartment. I have a security deposit. So why don't we both go to the sink. I won't make any false moves, and you can wash your damn hands."

She moved me along to the sink in the kitchen and she washed one hand at a time, still keeping the gun on me. I just stood a distance a way. "Use as many paper towels as you want," I said.

We went back to the main room. "Why did you kill Holbright?"

She shook her head. "Because it seemed easier than dealing with him. He was such a whiny, useless man. He looked good on camera, but he was not able to see the picture we were trying to paint."

` "You did it yourself? You didn't have Walter Benfress's goons do it like they did the others?"

She frowned, caught herself and then put on a small smile. "His goons are all gone. Arrested or dead. It's been crazy the last few days. Benfress is off. Somewhere with no extradition. He won't be found. He is the only one that no one will touch. Rich people have it so easy."

"Which is why you wanted the pill to make you rich," I said.

"Yes. I worked for him for years. And I wanted what he had. I let him put me in this dumb world of FlipSwitchers. Late night tv shows. But I thought the pill was going to work. I thought it could jump from illegal drugs to the world of supplements. I could have had Holbright sell them. It would have made me rich."

"Holbright too."

"The hell with Holbright. He is as dead as everyone else. I am sure you could reanimate him and have a nice conversation, but that's not going to happen."

I looked at her and then I got it. "Oh. That's why you're here. You were afraid I was going to reanimate him." She nodded. I was happy to understand things. I was happy things were going to be done. Some way. Things were going to be done soon.

She raised the gun. "You want to come with me and have me set you up with a television contract and a brand new life? I didn't think so."

A gun cracked. Janice collapsed. She bled on my floor. She made a mess of everything. Some people are like that.

In the doorway I saw Fisk. He was red faced and breathing hard. The gun was still aimed at where Janice was standing. He lowered the gun. "Now remember, you are in a lot of shock, Tim. But I need you to remember what happened."

"What happened?"

"I came in and told her to put the gun down and she refused and only then did I shoot. Do you remember that?"

"Yes. I remember that."

He came in and sat on the closest chair. "Three damn flights. I came to ask you to ratwarm Holbright. He's dead."

"Yeah. She told me."

I walked over to the dead publicist. I held her hand. I pushed. Her eyes burst open.

"Why the hell did you do that?" Fisk asked.

I ignored him. "Janice. Speak a little for me."

"Speak a little. Little dream. Dream a little dream of fields. Fields of wheat, Cream of wheat. This is part of a healthy breakfast." And then I took the spark away and she was gone again and for good.

I went to the kitchen and got a glass of water and gave it to Fisk. "Just water?" he asked. But he took it and drank it. The color in his face returned to something like normal.

"You're right, Fisk," I said. "They don't say anything. It's just nonsense. This ratwarming thing is for the birds."

He laughed. "That's what I been saying."

Seventeen

Maddin and Fisk took me out of my apartment the next week to make sure i was eating. "I didn't know you had babysitting duty."

Maddin said, "We get all the lousy jobs." They took him to a brightly lit Cafe with hanging plants and cloth napkins.

"Why are we at a place where the spoons are clean and not covered in grease?" I asked.

Maddin sighed. "Because my wife met my doctor in the supermarket and he told her that I had to eat better. And no cigars. What the hell."

"Meeting people in super markets never ends well," Fisk said.

"So now I am eating salads." And he was. A large garden salad was placed in front of him. And Maddin proceeded to put a jar of mayonnaise on it. "See. Healthy."

"Why am I here?" I asked.

"To eat. You need to be healthy too," Fisk said.

"Fine. But why am I here?"

Fisk and Maddin looked at each other and Fish spoke. "You need to come back to the station. It's been a week."

"I had a publicist point a gun at me. I have psychological damage."

"You do at that, but you came with it." Fisk said.

"You never were well put together," Maddin added.

"It's not like I do anything. It's not like I solve crimes. Why would I even want to bother."

Fisk smiled. "Like I said when it was all going down. You are our useless freak. We like having you around."

"No you don't."

"You a mind reader now? You got switched from one FlipSwitch power to another?"

"That's not how it works," I said.

"And you sitting on your ass doing nothing, feeling sorry for yourself that you ain't a saint of crime solving. Get over yourself and come back to work."

I had a tuna melt and it tasted right. I lingered on the fries that were not as crisp as I would have liked, but any fries are better than no fries. You have to accept the fate you are served. "But ratwarming doesn't work. Just another laughing stock."

"Like being a cop ain't a fixture of jeering," Maddin said quietly. "Look. You helped out last week. You did things I don't get."

"No. It would have worked out with me or without me."

"That's crap, Tim," Maddin said. "Everyone could say it. Take me out of the picture and it is still a picture. But that's not how it works. That's not how it should be. We need you because you might help."

"You want me around for the slight possibility that I could help out?"

"We are all living on the floor of possibility," Fisk said.

"What?" Maddin said, staring at his partner. "The hell did that mean? That means nothing. You made no sense."

Fisk was going to say something but his phone buzzed. "Crime calling. We got to go."

Maddin threw money on the table. "You coming Timmy?"

"Like a member of the team?" I asked.

"Don't go crazy. More like an eager kid brother. You coming? Dead people ain't waiting for long." Maddin laughed at his own joke and headed for the door with Fisk behind him.

They stopped at the door, looking at me still seated at the table.

"Come on."

Eighteen

"They others are gone, Aggie. It's just us."

"Can I trust you, Tim? I don't have my eyes. Are we alone."

"Yeah. We are alone. No one wanted to go. No one saw a reanimated corpse talk like you are talking."

"I am unique."

"You always were."

"I was killed brutally."

"You going to tell me about it? Help me solve your crime, Aggie?"

"I don't have anything to tell you. And even if I did, I don't think I would. There is something about this moment that makes me just want to talk to you and not follow whatI am expected to do."

"Who killed you Aggie?"

"How are you, Tim?"

"I'm alright."

"That's not true. You sound awful."

"It's a long day. And the corpse of my sister's ex-girlfriend is in front of me, talking to me."

"We should have done this while I was alive."

"That was me. I really didn't have much to say."

"Do you still have the watch?"

"What watch?"

"You know what watch. The Watch Kathy gave you."

"You got it for me. Kathy had no taste."

"She had taste. She dated me."

"No taste for jewelry. Come on Aggie. You are dead and now you are giving me a hard time?"

"Not going to get another chance."

"I still have the watch."

"You wearing it now?"

"I could lie and say yes. But no. It's back at the apartment."

"You kept it. I'm glad. I spent a lot of time looking for the right one."

"Any watch from the two of you was the right one."

"Kathy did not die because of me, you know."

"How would you know?

"I'm sorry. I didn't mean to upset you."

"I'm not upset. But you wouldn't know. How would anyone know."

"Well, I always thought you blamed me. That us not being together led her to killing herself."

"Sounds logical."

"She broke up with me."

"No she didn't."

"I wish we had a chance to talk about this. But she was so upset with me, she forbid me to talk to you."

"I guess you couldn't talk to me until you were dead."

"I guess so."

"She was sick. She was ill. I loved her. I love her. And she was having a hard time."

"And she jumped into the river."

"Not your fault, Tim."

"Not yours either, it seems."

"We all could have done more. I guess. I have never forgotten the last conversation we had, she and I. It broke my heart."

"What was the conversation?"

"Uh."

"You don't want to tell me?"

"I don't remember. I can't remember any of it."

"It happens."

"No. Not with this. I replayed that conversation every day of my life. And now that I am not. It's gone."

"Life is cruel."

"Death is cruel."

"Same thing. If you are talking, then you are alive."

"Without the memories that mean something to me. That's dead."

"Tell you what. I will try to remember you as well as I can. Will that do?"

"No. But thanks. I worry for you."

"You don't have to."

"I wish you had a goal. I wish you had something to make you happy."

"Being happy is overrated."

"Tim."

"It is. I miss my sister. When I get a chance, I will miss you too."

"I appreciate it."

"I wish we talked before it was too late."

"Oh. Speaking of too late. Things are going to get weirder for you."

"What?"

"Dom, my husband, is going to be dead soon. And others are going to be dead soon. There is going to be a lot of death."

"How do you know that?"

"I don't know. How am I talking to you right now? Do we really need to understand things?"

"Okay. Thanks."

"But you are not going to tell anyone what I said?"

"Nope."

"Why? I'm giving you a heads up."

"Because this conversation is mine. I am not sharing it with anyone. I never said goodbye to Kathy. I am going to say goodbye to you. And I am not going to share it. Mine. Let me be selfish. Let me have something that no one else has."

"Don't let me stop you."

"Goodbye Aggie. I'm glad we chatted."

"Goodbye Tim. I'm glad we chatted."

"You can go. I'll take it from here."

The book was completed February 14, 2023 -DM

A Note from the Writer

If you liked this book, you might want to try "Tales from The Reanimator's Saloon," available as an eBook. It is a collection of stories that take place in O. Onions. The same regulars show up. Tim even shows up for one story, though it really is not the same. This book, Ratwarmer, is its own creature and I am proud of its individuality. But give the earlier book a shot. I don't know if that makes this a series. It might. I'm not sure. There might be a third book. I have an idea I might pursue. Of course, this book, Ratwarmer, took five years to write. Sort of. I wrote the first four fifths in 2018 over the course of several months. And then, nothing until yesterday. Now, February of 2023, I figured I would plow through and finish it. And here we are. So the third book might be done in the next decade. Keep your eyes out for it.

About the Book

Tim is a ratwarmer.

He has the power to bring people back from the dead.

During the FlipSwitch, some people got some powers. Tim got the power of reanimation.

It's not as great as it seems.

He works for the police. He brings recently dead victims back so they can be a witness to their own death. That's what a ratwarmer does.

It doesn't work well, but it's worth a try.

Now, there is a murder in town. The wife a wealthy man. Tim knew this woman. And now he will have to bring her back.

There is a world of corruption that only the dead know and Tim can get them to talk.

There is a dead body so it's a mystery. People have strange powers so it is a fantasy. There are reanimated bodies, so it also could be a horror.

But what it is, is the story of a guy not sure of his place in the world. A strange world, but it is the only we he has.

About the Writer

David has written over a 100 eBooks. Most of them are short, but some of them are pretty okay. His short novels include: Funny Animals, Delivery, The Truth Seeker, More Sopping Products, Well Remembered Movies, Third Floor Office, among others. He has several short story collections: Not a Day of Miracles, Martha and Emily, The Further Adventures of Polly Mintslab, Little Adventures, among a bunch of others. He has put out three eZine series: Comic Book Hinterland, The Long Weekend Review and Argle Bargle. He writes a monthly column in Worcester Review. For over a decade, he was the host of a popular poetry reading series in Worcester. He would love to hear from you.

www.ingramcontent.com/pod-product-compliance
Lightning Source LLC
Chambersburg PA
CBHW021750150726
47989CB00004B/1587